Library of Congress Cataloging in Publication
Number: 2017951338

ISBN: 978-1-68369-116-7

Printed in China

Typeset in Futura and Miller

Designed by Doogie Horner
Illustrated by Kim Smith
Production management by John J. McGurk

Quirk Books
215 Church Street
Philadelphia, PA 19106
quirkbooks.com

10 9 8 7 6 5 4 3 2 1

BACK TO THE FUTURE

Based on the movie written by
ROBERT ZEMECKIS & BOB GALE
Illustrated by KIM SMITH

QUIRK BOOKS
PHILADELPHIA

This is Marty McFly.

It is 1985 and Marty lives in a town called Hill Valley.

Hill Valley is a friendly town with a courthouse
that's famous because of its broken clock.

The clock stopped thirty years ago, after it was struck by lightning. Today, the people of Hill Valley want to make sure the clock is preserved.

Marty's best friend is a scientist named Doctor Emmett Brown. Marty calls him Doc.

Doc is always making cool inventions, like an automatic dog food feeder . . .

EINSTEIN

. . . and a giant guitar amplifier!

But Marty's life at home is not so cool.

Marty's parents, George and Lorraine, don't seem to love each other.

His brother Dave and his sister Linda are always arguing.

And George has a mean
boss named Biff Tannen.

Biff is a bully. He always
pushes George around and
makes him do extra work.

Marty wishes his father would stand up to Biff,
but George doesn't have the courage.

newest invention to Marty.

He's built a time machine—
in a car!

"The way I see it," Doc explains, "if you're
going to build a time machine into a car,
why not do it with some style?"

The time machine uses a special fuel called plutonium.

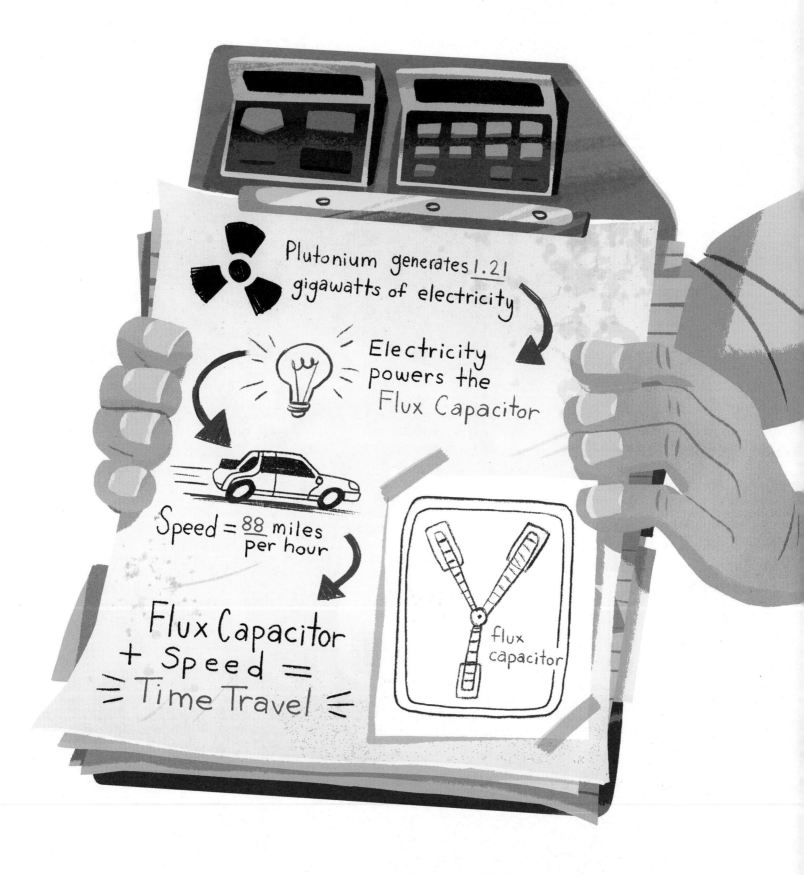

When Marty test-drove the time machine . . .

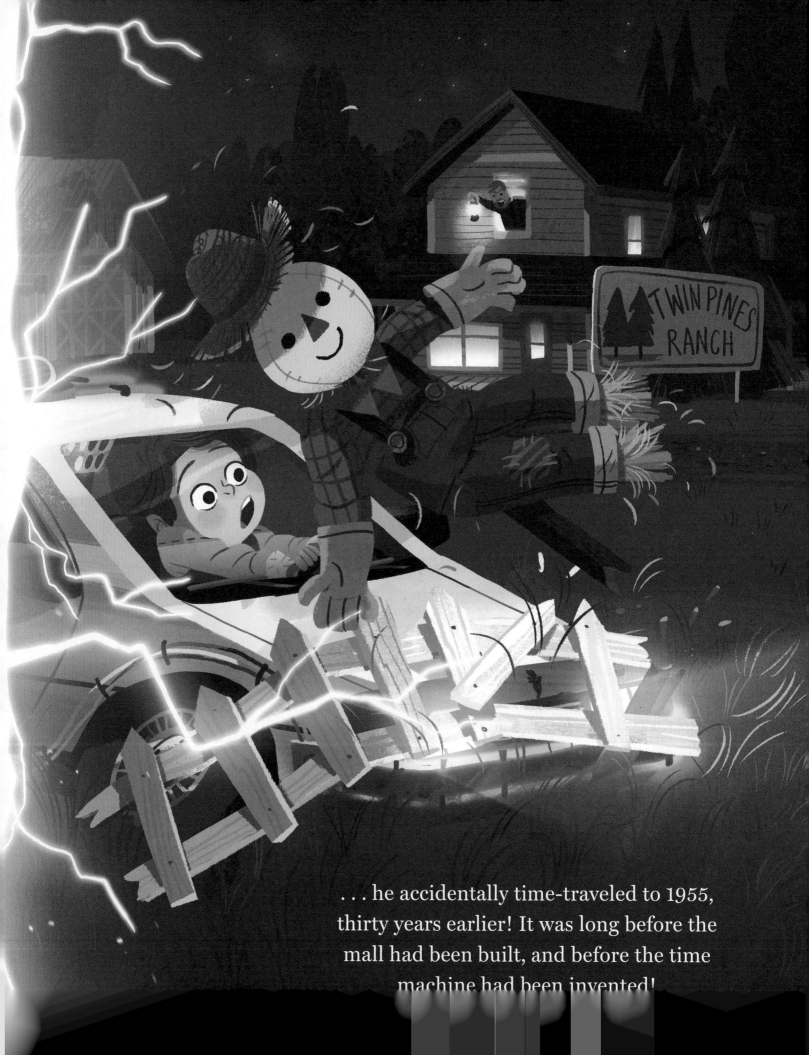

. . . he accidentally time-traveled to 1955,
thirty years earlier! It was long before the
mall had been built, and before the time
machine had been invented!

Marty knew he had to get home, so he hid the time machine and went to search for young Doc Brown. Hopefully the time machine's inventor could help him get back to the future.

Marty discovered that Hill Valley looked very different in 1955.

The cars looked different.

The clothes looked different.

But the clock was working fine because it was still one week before the lightning bolt would strike it.

Before Marty could find young
Doc Brown, he found his parents
at a soda shop. In 1955, George
and Lorraine were teenagers,
just like Marty!

And that bully Biff was still pushing poor George around and making him do his homework.

Marty defended George and accidentally interfered
with his parents' romance. Now Lorraine liked Marty
because he stood up to Biff!

This was a problem. If George and Lorraine didn't fall
in love and marry, how could they ever have kids?

Marty looked at a photo of himself with
his brother and sister. Dave and Linda
were starting to disappear . . . as if they'd
never been born!

Marty located the house of young Doc Brown and introduced himself. "My name is Marty and I'm from the future. I came here in a time machine that you invented, and now I need 1.21 gigawatts of electricity to get back to the year 1985." Doc didn't believe him.

So Marty took Doc to the time machine, but Doc had bad news. "There's no plutonium in 1955, and only a bolt of lightning can generate that kind of power. Unfortunately, we never know when or where lightning will strike."

Marty told Doc the story of the clock tower.
The lightning bolt would strike it in just a few days!

Doc quickly put together a plan. "If we can harness the energy from the lightning, we can send you back to the future!"

"But Marty," Doc says, "before you leave 1955, you have to make sure your parents fall in love. Otherwise, you and your brother and sister will never be born!"

Marty spent the next few days trying to make his parents fall in love.

Marty begged George to invite Lorraine to the school dance. Though George liked Lorraine, he was too shy to ask her.

Marty checked the photo again and saw that he was starting to fade away too! He had to do something!

Marty remembered that his father liked science fiction. So that night, Marty sneaked into George's bedroom dressed like an alien.

"I am Darth Vader from Planet Vulcan!" Marty said. "If you don't invite Lorraine to the school dance, I will melt your brain!"

The trick worked! George found the courage to speak to Lorraine.

But Marty knew he'd also have to teach George to find the courage to stand up for himself.

Things worked out perfectly.
George liked Lorraine so much
that he stood up for her to
protect her from Biff.

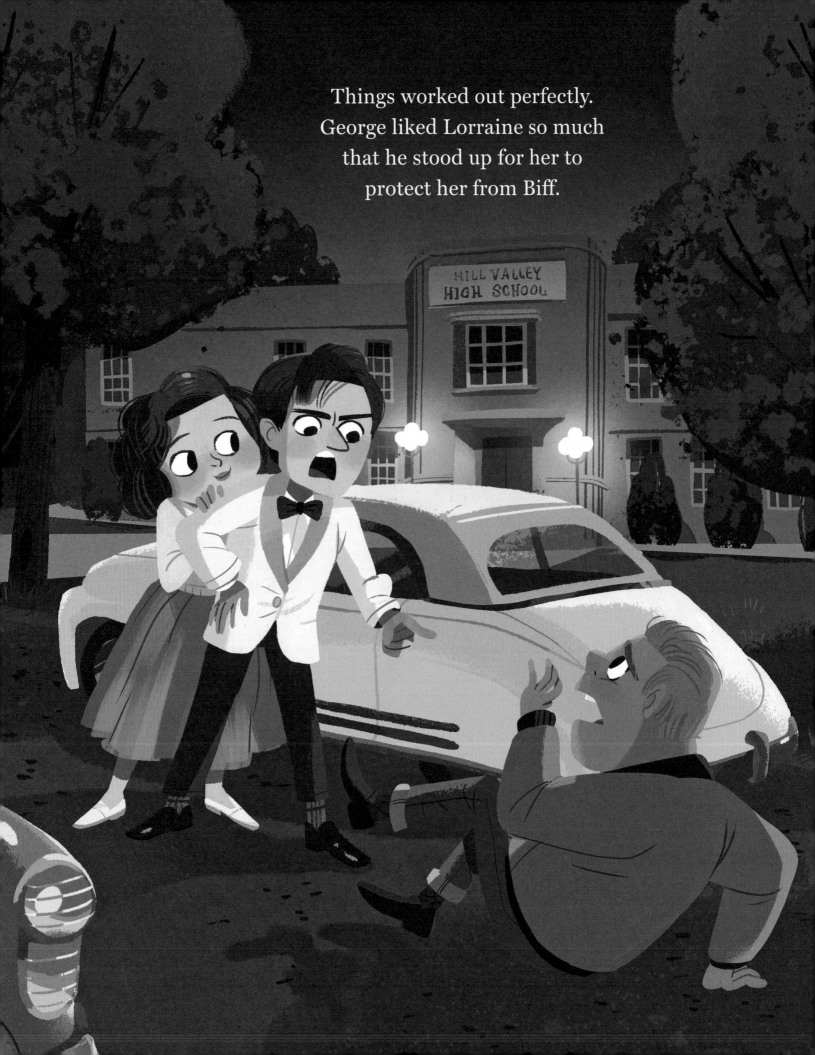

And that night, George and Lorraine danced, kissed, and fell in love. Marty's plan worked!

And just in time too! Because that very night, lightning was going to strike the clock tower. Doc put his plan in motion. He attached a giant wire to the clock . . .

. . . while Marty raced down the street, speeding up to 88 miles per hour.

Doc connected the cables just as Marty drove under them and lightning struck the clock tower!

The electricity powered the Flux Capacitor,
and the time machine returned to 1985.

Marty was safe in his own time.

Now, because George had learned to stand up for himself, things at home were very different. George and Lorraine loved each other.

His brother Dave and his sister Linda didn't argue anymore.

I'm almost finished waxing your car, Mr. McFly.

And Biff never bullied George again. In fact, now Biff worked for George!

George even published a science-fiction novel! It was based on a dream he had when he was just a teenager. At least, George *thought* it was a dream.

A MATCHMADE in SPACE

GEORGE MCFLY

From that day on, Marty and Doc
had many more exciting adventures
. . . in the past, present, and future.